Today Is

a traditional song
retold by Ruby Mae

illustrated by
Nadine Bernard Westcott

HARCOURT BRACE & COMPANY

Orlando   Atlanta   Austin   Boston   San Francisco   Chicago   Dallas   New York
Toronto   London

Today is Monday.
Today is Monday.
Monday art day.
Everybody happy?
Well, I should say!

Today is Tuesday.
Today is Tuesday.
Tuesday snow day.
Everybody happy?
Well, I should say!

Today is Wednesday.
Today is Wednesday.
Wednesday music day.
Everybody happy?
Well, I should say!

Today is Thursday.
Today is Thursday.
Thursday birthday.
Everybody happy?
Well, I should say!

Today is Friday.
Today is Friday.
Friday sharing day.
Everybody happy?
Well, I should say!

Today is Saturday.
Today is Saturday.
Saturday play day.
Everybody happy?
Well, I should say!

Today is Sunday.
Today is Sunday.
Sunday rest day.
Everybody happy?
Wasn't that fun!